Little Rabbit Lost

HARRY HORSE

PUFFIN BOOKS

For Jessica and Ben

PUFFIN BOOKS
Published by the Penguin Group
Penguin Books Ltd, 80 Strand, London WC2R 0RL, England
Penguin Putnam Inc., 375 Hudson Street, New York, New York 10014, USA
Penguin Books Australia Ltd, 250 Camberwell Road, Camberwell, Victoria 3124, Australia
Penguin Books Canada Ltd, 10 Alcorn Avenue, Toronto, Ontario, Canada M4V 3B2
Penguin Books India (P) Ltd, 11 Community Centre, Panchsheel Park, New Delhi – 110 017, India
Penguin Books (NZ) Ltd, Cnr Rosedale and Airborne Roads, Albany, Auckland, New Zealand
Penguin Books (South Africa) (Pty) Ltd, 24 Sturdee Avenue, Rosebank 2196, South Africa

Penguin Books Ltd, Registered Offices: 80 Strand, London WC2R 0RL, England

www.penguin.com

First published 2002
1 3 5 7 9 10 8 6 4 2

Text and illustrations copyright © Harry Horse, 2002

The moral right of the author/illustrator has been asserted

Set in Cochin 18/26pt

Manufactured in China

British Library Cataloguing in Publication Data
A CIP catalogue record for this book is available from the British Library

ISBN 0–670–89989–5

Little Rabbit woke up
and knew it was a special
day. "It's my birthday," he
said. "I'm not such a little
rabbit any more!"

He hopped out of bed and found a lovely pile of presents and
an enormous red balloon.

The whole family
watched as he
opened his presents.

"Happy birthday,
Little Rabbit!" they
cheered. "And one
more surprise …"

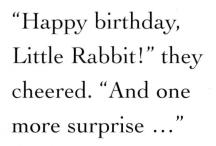

"Tickets for Rabbit World. For all of us!"
Little Rabbit had wanted to go to Rabbit
World for as long as he could remember.
He was *very* excited.

Mama packed a special birthday picnic,
and soon everyone was ready to go.

They set off for
Rabbit World with
Little Rabbit and his red
balloon leading the way.

Little Rabbit led them across the fields.
"Don't go too far!" called Papa.

"But it's my birthday and I'm a big rabbit now,"
shouted Little Rabbit, and he ran ahead anyway.

Little Rabbit suddenly stopped at the top
of a hill and everyone caught up with him.
"Look!" said Little Rabbit. "It's Rabbit
World! It's huge!" and off he ran again.

CARROT SPEEDBOATS

BOUNCY CASTLE

BIG HOPPER

Once they were all inside Rabbit World,
Little Rabbit couldn't decide what to do first.
He wanted to go on everything at once.

"Don't go too far!" called Mama. "There are lots of rabbits here and you might get lost. Stay close."

"But it's my birthday and I'm a big rabbit now," said Little Rabbit. "I won't get lost."

Little Rabbit quickly ran off ahead, past the pirate ship and carrot speedboats. There was so much to see and do!

"Mama, can you push me on
the big swings? Can I go on
the climbing frame?"

"I'm sorry, Little Rabbit, but
you're too small. You can go
on the helter-skelter though,"
said Mama.

"That is for babies, Mama. It's my birthday and I'm a big rabbit now. I want to go on that!" said Little Rabbit, pointing …

… to the Big Hopper.

"I'm sorry, Little Rabbit, but you're too small," said Mama. So Little Rabbit had to watch his brothers and sisters zoom past instead.

Little Rabbit soon got bored watching. "It's not fair," he said to himself. "It's my birthday and I *am* a big rabbit. Why can't I go on the really fun rides like everyone else?"

"Wow!" said Little Rabbit.
"I wonder if my new rocket
will fly that fast?"

"Hooray! A bouncy castle! Even *I'm* allowed to go
on this." And so Little Rabbit clambered on and
bounced and hopped and nearly took off until –

"Oh," said Little Rabbit.
"Where's Mama? And
Papa?" He suddenly felt
as small as he really was.

Little Rabbit asked some bigger rabbits, "Have you seen my mama?"

And he asked some grown-up rabbits.

But nobody had seen
Little Rabbit's mama.

"Has anyone seen my mama?" said Little Rabbit.

Little Rabbit began to cry.
He was all alone and didn't
know what to do.

Other rabbits gathered
round, asking him lots
of questions about his
mama. And then,
through all the voices
he heard …

"Little Rabbit! There you are. We've been so worried!"

It was Mama. "Thank goodness for your red balloon! I thought we might never find you." Little Rabbit was so happy he cried a bit more.

"I'm sorry, Mama. I *am* still your Little Rabbit. I'll stay close now," said Little Rabbit.

"Come on, I think we've all had enough of Rabbit World for one day," said Mama.

The Rabbit family settled down to enjoy
Little Rabbit's birthday picnic. Little Rabbit
made sure he stayed very close to Mama.
"Just one last surprise ..." said Mama.

"Happy birthday, Little Rabbit!"